QUIT? NOT ME!

A Story of Dependability

By Raymond & Dorothy Moore
Illustrated by Julie Downing

THOMAS NELSON PUBLISHERS
Nashville • Camden • New York

Quit? Not Me!

Published in Nashville, Tennessee, by Thomas Nelson, Inc., and distributed in
Canada by Lawson Falle, Ltd., Cambridge, Ontario.

Printed in the United States of America

ISBN 0-8407-6652-1

Every Tuesday I take care of my little brother, Jamie, after school. Mom has this class she goes to at the Y. But this Tuesday I forgot. My friend, Davey, and I got to shooting baskets in the alley. Suddenly I remembered, and Davey and I took off.

"Jamie will be scared," I worried.

When we reached my house, Grandpa Bush leaned over his porch railing. "Jamie is over here, John," he called. His friend, Grandpa Ray, was on the porch, too, with Jamie on his lap.

"You forgotten me!" Jamie sobbed. "I was scared!"

Before I could say I was sorry, Grandpa Bush lit into me. "You can't depend on anybody these days. Especially kids."

Grandpa Ray dried Jamie's tears. "Not like the good old days," he said. "Our folks could depend on us."

The grandpas were ganging up on me. So I defended myself. "Everyone forgets once in a while, even adults."

But Grandpa Bush kept it up. "I'll bet neither of you boys can do what you're told for one whole day — let alone for one hour after school."

"Sure we can!" I said without thinking. "We can do anything for one day!"

At that Grandpa Bush slapped his knee. "Is that a promise, young fella? Grandpa Ray and I can think up a humdinger of a test to see just how prompt and dependable you are."

"I - I - I don't know . . ." Davey stammered.

"I promise!" I boomed.

I really thought Grandpa Bush was joking. But two days later he called from his yard, "It's all set for tomorrow. Be on my porch at eight o'clock sharp. Being on time is part of the test."

Grandpa Ray told Davey the same thing.

"Why do they want us so early?" Davey asked. "What will we have to do?"

"There's only one way to find out," I said. "Be there!"

I like to sleep late in the summertime. But I couldn't quit before I even started. I made it to Grandpa Bush's front steps at exactly eight. On the top step I found a note under a brick.

This might be fun, I thought. I like surprises. Then I read the note. WEED YOUR MOTHER'S GARDEN, it said. WHEN YOU ARE DONE, LOOK IN THE BIRD FEEDER.

"Oh, no! I hate weeding!" I kicked a can as I clomped home. The weeds in the garden were taller than the plants. The soil was wet from an early morning rain. It wasn't fair.

My neck was aching after I'd weeded only half a row. My shoes and pant legs were caked with mud. I was ready to quit when I saw a fat, wiggly earthworm under a leaf. Then I saw two more. Mr. Long pays fifty cents a dozen for fishing worms. I went back to the house to get a big plastic bucket. Each time I uncovered an earthworm, I dropped it in the container. By the end of the fourth row I had four dozen worms. And the weeding was done!

I felt good. I could hardly wait to tell Davey I'd found two dollars worth of worms while keeping my promise. Then I took the second note out of the bird feeder.

CLEAN GRANDPA BUSH'S GARAGE, the note said. WHEN YOU ARE DONE, GO HOME AND EAT LUNCH.

Clean the garage! I should have known the second job would be harder than the first. Grandpa Bush's garage was full of junk. He parked his old truck in the driveway.

I'd just opened the garage door when Grandpa Bush got in his truck. "I've got business downtown. Do a good job," he said.

I fumed as I watched him drive off. Why couldn't he clean his own garage? I sat down on the barrel. I could just picture Davey over at Grandpa Ray's. Grandpa Ray kept his garage clean as anything.

I began by moving stuff out on the driveway. Then I pounded some large nails into the wall studs for hangers. Shovels, rakes, brooms, ropes, and hoses. I hung things up and out of the way as fast as I could.

Some of the other stuff was really interesting. In one corner I uncovered an old popcorn popper. It had a round pan with a wire cover and a long, long handle. My dad liked to tell about popping corn in the fireplace when he was a boy. Next I discovered a large wooden pail with a crank handle. Faded letters on the side spelled ICE CREAM.

The things I couldn't hang up, I stacked in piles. Magazines and papers went in one pile. Old rags and rugs went in another. At last I swept the dirt out the front door. I had never worked so hard in my whole life!

Good job, I thought as I closed the door. And now I was supposed to go home for lunch. My stomach was ready for that.

But when I opened the bread box, there it was! Another note! CLEAN UP THE KITCHEN, it said. AT 3:00 RIDE OUT TO THE OLD SCHOOLHOUSE.

I leaned against the refrigerator. Dishes! I hate doing dishes worse than I hate weeding! And now the sink, the table, and the counter were stacked with dirty dishes. Where was Mom anyway? Had she and Grandpa Bush carted dishes in from the whole neighborhood?

I made myself a sandwich and poured a glass of milk. It was just past one o'clock. If I wasn't at the schoolhouse by three, it would prove Grandpa Bush was right: I couldn't do what I was told for one whole day. I had to keep my promise.

I decided to make a game out of this last job. First I scraped the dirty dishes. Then I put my new record on the stereo. Next I filled the sink with hot soapy water. Then I played the record with the volume turned up. No one was at home to complain.

I washed dishes in time to the music. Scrub, scrub, rinse. Scrub, scrub, rinse. The record played three more times before the dishes were done. I drank another glass of milk and left for the old schoolhouse. I wondered if I'd meet Davey on the way.

At three o'clock sharp, I rode into the schoolyard. I'd just gotten off my bike when the schoolhouse doors burst open.

"Hurrah, John!" "Good for John!" "John did it!" Almost everyone in the neighborhood was there. And they were all cheering for me! Grandpa Ray shook my hand. Allie, Trina, and Nika were there along with Ken and Pedro. I didn't see Davey.

"How'd you like to join the Schoolhouse Gang?" Allie asked.

"Schoolhouse Gang? What's that?"

"We meet here at the schoolhouse to plan how to help people," Grandpa Ray said. "We need dependable kids like you, John."

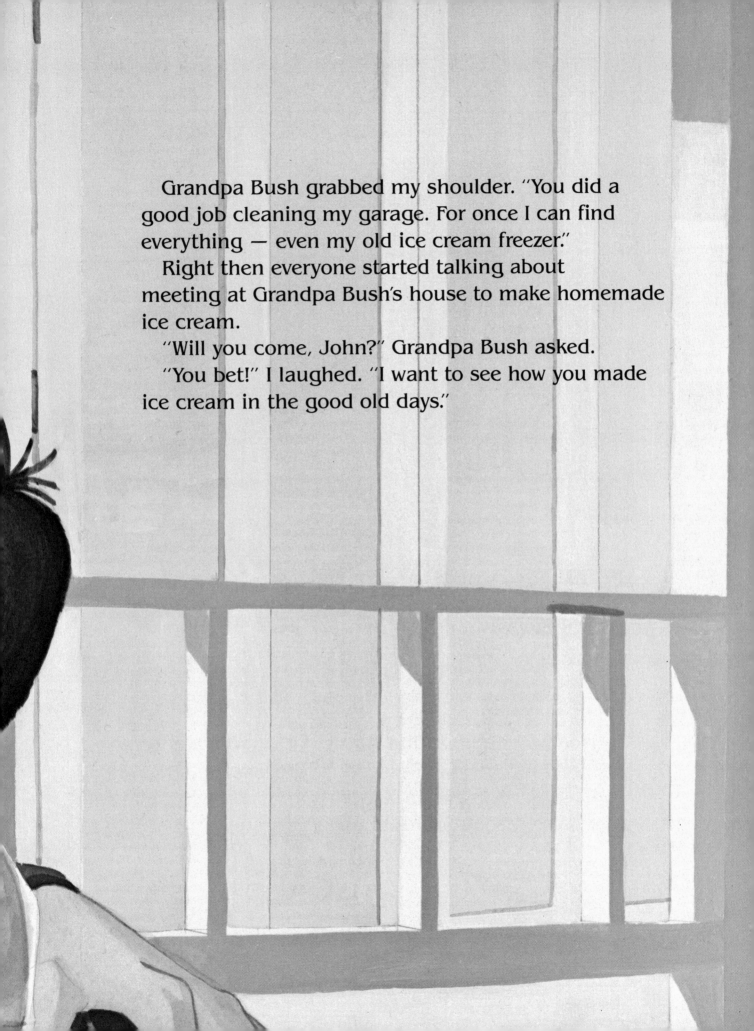

Grandpa Bush grabbed my shoulder. "You did a good job cleaning my garage. For once I can find everything — even my old ice cream freezer."

Right then everyone started talking about meeting at Grandpa Bush's house to make homemade ice cream.

"Will you come, John?" Grandpa Bush asked.

"You bet!" I laughed. "I want to see how you made ice cream in the good old days."

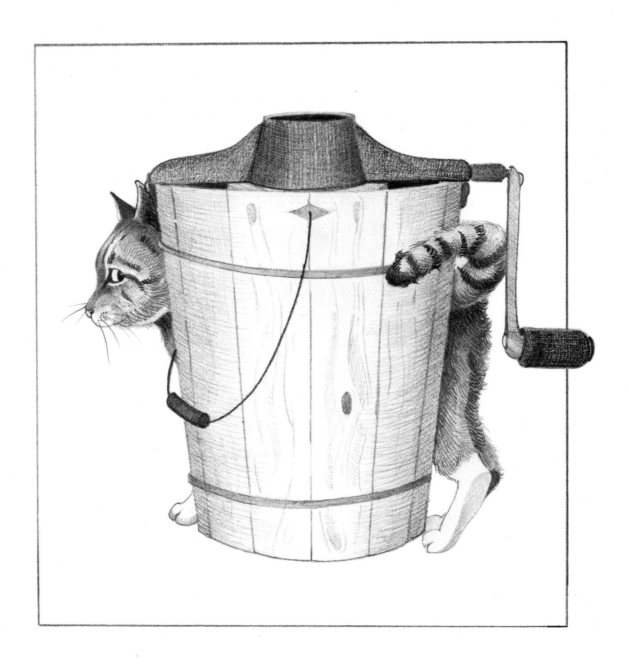

I found out later that Davey got up too late to even start the dependability test. Maybe Grandpa Ray will give him another chance. I'm sure glad I kept my promise without quitting ahead of time.

Letter to Parents

Children seldom realize how important the trait of dependability is to themselves and to others. Dorothy and I like to begin our discussion of this trait with an example from nature, since we depend upon the natural world more than we realize.

For instance, we navigate our planes and ships by the sun and stars. We set our clocks by the sun. Children always enjoy hearing how this is done, and the explanation shows how much we depend on nature — and other persons. The sun is always on time.

Each day the clocks of Western Union, which are electrically controlled, are connected to the U. S. Naval Observatory in Washington, D. C. At five seconds before noon, a warning "tick" sounds over the wires. Then, at the exact instant the sun is over the meridian, a technician at the Naval Observatory flashes a signal over the wires, and every Western Union clock is automatically set for the day.

Just as we depend on the sun and the technicians at Western Union, other people depend on us. When we are late, we often make others late. Sometimes we interrupt meetings or make people rush, which can cause accidents.

After you have discussed this material with your children, ask them to describe times people depended on them. What would have happened if they'd been undependable?

Now discuss the story with them. What happened when John wasn't dependable? How did he pass the dependability test? If your children don't have any ideas, remind them that John made a job he disliked more tolerable by collecting worms to sell as bait. Dish washing became less a chore when he listened to his favorite record. Developing our own system of rewards is part of learning dependability and self-motivation.

None of us can expect our children to develop dependable habits on their own. Dorothy and I have used three different vehicles to encourage dependability in youngsters. They are: (1) work activities *with* us; (2) service to others; and (3) tests or checks to see how they are doing. The methods vary according to the child's age.

Before six. Chores done *with* you can be your most effective behavior tool. In fact, if preschoolers do such things *with you,* they will often enjoy work as much as they enjoy play. If you have several children, have the older child help the younger. Or have the entire family work as a team, which often increases creative interaction among family members. Be sure to openly show your appreciation for your children's work.

Preschoolers need to exercise their large muscles (their legs and arms) and to practice using their small muscles (such as their fingers), which are not yet well coordinated. You might keep these needs in mind as you plan their work/play activities.

At six and seven. If you have done your homework, young children are beginning to accept such responsibilities as doing dishes, cleaning their rooms, and feeding their pets. They are beginning to understand more consistently *why* they must be dependable, but they continue to need your positive emotional support.

Chores help a child feel needed and depended upon. This self-worth makes them independent from their peers, and helps them to avoid the social cancer of peer dependency, which often robs them of traditional moral values.

At eight and nine. By this time, children are learning to reason consistently and can be depended upon to bring independent thought to their tasks, as long as you are firm and consistent in your instructions. Children are now capable of fine muscle coordination, and are ready for unpressured training in manual skills.

Praise and encouragement from you, and frank answers to questions about impending changes — body development, sex — as they enter puberty is important to their development. Even though they are becoming more aware of their peers, they need to feel wanted and depended upon at home, so they can maintain a discreet independence from peer pressure. They enjoy being involved in projects that serve others.

Preadolescence. Children need continual counsel to understand impending physical and emotional changes and how to adjust to them. They are ready for carefully planned daily programs of responsibility, such as planting and caring for their own garden or doing the yard work, baby-sitting, or helping paint and fix up their rooms. But be careful about nagging or talking down to them.

The stories in the Schoolhouse Gang series are adapted from true experiences. We hope you will use them, as we have, to present basic Judeo-Christian character values to your children.

Raymond and Dorothy Moore

Every day the shiny silver plane flew over the little farm in the valley.

And every day Petunia, and Charley the gander,

and their goslings, watched . . .

until it vanished beyond the distant hills.

"Where does it come from?" asked the goslings. "Where does it go?"

"Ah, it comes from far away," said Petunia. "And it goes where the sky goes, far, far away. It must be nice, far away."

One day, Petunia said: "*Watch me!* I am going to fly up to the sky, like the plane, and see how big the world is beyond the hills. I will come back presently to tell you what I saw."

Petunia flapped her wings so furiously that the grasses bent their heads. But she rose no higher than the rabbit jumps, and then she fell on her head . . . *plump!*

"I know what's wrong with you," said Charley the gander.
"You are almost as fat as I am. Go and climb on the scale and
see."

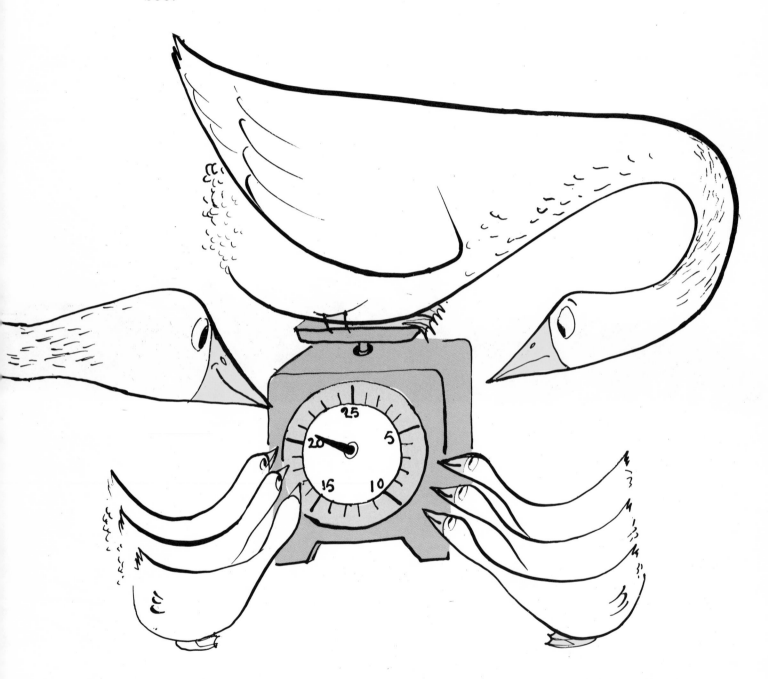

Petunia did see! "Twenty pounds!" she cried.
"Twenty pounds! Hoo . . . oo," cried the goslings.
"A twenty-pound goose can't fly to the sky," said Charley.

"Well," said Petunia, "I know what I'll do—
C-A-L-I-S-TH-E-N-I-C-S!
"Lots of CALISTHENICS; until I am light enough to fly."
And she did calisthenics in the middle of the farmyard, every
morning and every afternoon. Like this . . .

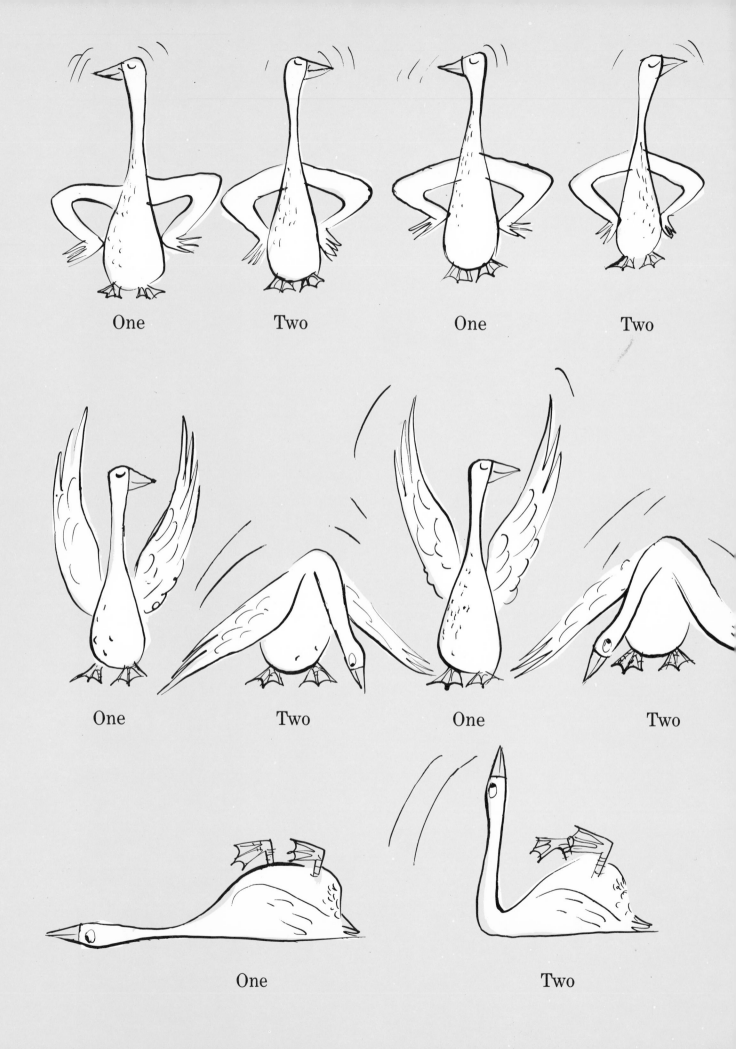

One

Two

One

Two

One

Two

One

Two

One

Two

One   Two

One   Two   One   Two

Before long Petunia was as slender as the guinea hen. She was strong, too—so strong that she decided the time had come to try her wings again.

She went to the meadow, and after a short run—*zoom!*—she climbed up on her great white wings.

It worked!

She climbed higher and higher, over the heads of her cheering friends . . .

. . . higher and higher over the little farm . . . and over the hills . . .
higher and higher until the earth below was like a soft green
rug, and tiny red and white dots were all she could see of the
farm buildings. She made sharp turns, right and left; she glided
like the eagle. She had the sky all to herself. It was wonderful.

But in her joy Petunia did not see the dark clouds coming toward her. Before she could flee, a high wind blew them all around her, lightning blinded her, and she was carried away by an angry storm. Blown about the black clouds like a leaf, she could not tell which way was up and which was down.

When at last the sky cleared, Petunia saw, far below, a very strange sight. The whole earth was laid with rows of houses set close together like stones in a wall. The rows opened only to let through two rivers full of busy boats.

"Oh, what an adventure," said Petunia, above the big city.
"Where am I? What am I going to do?" She was so tired she
simply let herself down and alighted at a street crossing.

Petunia was quite frightened at first. So many noises, so many people, so many cars—and so many windows above! Happily, as the policeman blew his whistle to stop the traffic, a taxi driver cried:

"Petunia! . . . It's Petunia!"

"A thousand whistles," said the policeman. "So it is."

The crowd pressed around Petunia to pet her, but the policeman and the taxi driver saw that she was hungry and tired and
they whisked her away in the taxicab to the cafeteria around the
corner.

While Petunia ate a triple-decker sandwich, the policeman and the taxi driver told her about their city, how beautiful and big it was.

"Why," said the policeman, "most houses are bigger than your farmhouse, barns, and silo put together."

"And wait," said the taxi driver. "You wouldn't believe it, even our animals are bigger." And they drove Petunia to a place where trees and grass grew and animals were kept. Indeed, city animals were not at all like those on the farm. Some were so tall—as tall as maypoles.

And Petunia felt smaller looking up at them . . .

smaller . . .   and smaller . . .

"Wait," said the policeman. "You have not seen the biggest
one." And they took Petunia to a house where an animal as large
as a barn stood quietly munching peanuts.

He was so big Petunia felt still smaller.

"Wait," said the taxi driver. "That's nothing. You haven't seen the boats in the city." And they drove Petunia to the riverside, where boats as big as hills were tied with ropes as big as trees. They were so big, Petunia felt still smaller.

"Wait," said the policeman. "You haven't seen the deepest
street in the city." And they drove Petunia to a street as deep as
a crevice in the mountain.

It was so deep, Petunia, at the bottom, felt still smaller.

"Wait," said the taxi driver. "You haven't seen the tallest house in the city." And they drove Petunia to a place where there was a house so tall that its roof was hidden in the clouds. So tall, Petunia felt still smaller. (She is the smaller dot in the right corner. The larger dots are the policeman, the taxi driver, and the taxicab.)

"Wait," said the policeman. "I will show you the house in which my wife and I live." And they drove Petunia to a house so big it would have held *all* the farmhouses in Petunia's village with their barns and their silos.

Petunia now felt so small she feared she was in danger of disappearing altogether. You cannot see her here. She is so small.

And she was worried to think she had shrunk so. She *must* return to her farm or there would be no more Petunia. But the policeman and Petunia thanked the taxi driver for the beautiful ride and they went up to the policeman's apartment.

In the apartment Petunia saw a sparrow picking crumbs on
the window sill and she felt at once a little bigger again.

"How can you live in the big city?" she asked him. "You are so
small! You would be happier on a farm."

"I don't like farms," said the sparrow. "There aren't enough
windows for crumbs. I manage very well here, thank you."

"You are so tiny anyway, it makes little difference, I suppose."

"Why don't you go back to your farm?" asked the sparrow.

"It's too far for me to fly. The storm blew me here, but it won't
blow me back to my farm."

"Sorry," said the busy sparrow, "but I see some crumbs over
there. Good-bye, Petunia."

The policeman's wife was glad to see Petunia. She cooked a
delicious dinner for her, and put her to sleep in a soft bed under
the television. But she knew that Petunia was not happy.

"She misses her farm," she told her husband. "We must put
her on the train tomorrow."

The next day the policeman and his wife took Petunia to a
railroad station so big it would have enclosed a mountain. They
kissed Petunia and Petunia waved to them when the train
started off.

"Come and visit me in the country!" she cried to her kind
friends.

From her seat by the train window, Petunia watched the green fields, the *small* houses, the *small* streams, as they glided by, and she felt more and more like a real-size goose again. She was happy.

"It's good to go home," she said to herself.

In the *small* station of her village, she was greeted by
Charley, the goslings, and all her normal-size farmyard friends.
And that night she slept happily in her normal-size house.

Many a time afterward she told her children about the beautiful, big, *big* world one could see beyond the hills.

ROGER DUVOISIN

is widely recognized as one of the foremost
author-illustrators of children's books of this
century. He was born in Geneva in 1904 and
worked as an artist in Switzerland and France
before coming to this country in the early
1930s to design silks for an American textile
firm. His first book, *A Little Boy Is Drawing*,
which he made as a gift to his young son, was
published in 1932. In the years since then,
until his death in 1980, he illustrated forty
books that he had written, and more than a
hundred books by other authors, among them
The Happy Lion and its sequels, written by
Louise Fatio, his wife. Throughout his career
he won many awards, including the Caldecott
Medal in 1947 for *White Snow, Bright Snow*
by Alvin Tresselt, and a Caldecott Honor in
1966 for *Hide and Seek*, also by Tresselt. He
is perhaps best remembered now for his
gently humorous picture books featuring such
distinctive animal characters as Veronica, the
conspicuous hippopotamus, and, most
notably, Petunia, the silly goose.